CORAL RUMBLE

LITTLE LIGHT

ILLUSTRATIONS BY SHIH-YU LIN

Published by TROIKA

First published 2021

Troika Books Ltd, Well House,

Green Lane, Ardleigh CO7 7PD, UK

www.troikabooks.com

A CIP catalogue record for this book is available

from the British Library

ISBN 978-1-912745-16-6

1 3 5 7 9 10 8 6 4 2

Printed and bound in Great Britain by Clay's Ltd,

Elcograf S.p.A.

In memory of Harold Edward Woodwards
(1899–1991)
Grandad, to me.
My very own 'Nana' character,
in troubled times.

CONTENTS

Nothing can dim the light that shines from within.
Maya Angelou

HOTEL LIVING

HiDiNG

I'm hiding,
I'm good at hiding.
Have been all my life.

Where are you, Ava?
Mum would shout
and shout
until I heard
the cracks
in her patience
snap open.

But she's not here in the market square,
where I'm hiding under tarpaulin,
hiding under this covered
wobbly market stall table,
watching for their feet,
wishing for their feet
to keep running.

HOLDING BREATH

I count their feet.
There are ten.
They're all standing
the other side of
this tarpaulin.

Where is she?
asks one girl.
Let's split up,
search around,
suggests a boy.
They all agree,
laugh the kind of
laughs that feed
on the misery
of others.

I count their feet
leaving, two by two,
until no feet remain
the other side of
this tarpaulin.

PHEW!

CAKE STEALING

I'm good at cake stealing.
Have never felt guilty
about the sugar
on my lips.

of my day
the cherry on the top
cake stealing has always been

of my life
the icing on the top
cake stealing has always been

I'm good at cake stealing,
it's how I celebrate.
Today I celebrate
running feet.

THE PARK

I sit on a swing
to finish my cake,
then push off
with my feet,
toes pointing out
like jousting lances
my hands sticky
against cool chains
head thrown back
eyes softly closed
and swing
and swing
and swing
and swing
and swing

until the rhythm
slows,
drops into
stillness.

I sit,
motionless,
apart for my
darting
                eyes
looking
                out
for
                THEM.

BACK TO THE HOTEL

Some children go on holiday,
they pack a case and drive away
to big hotels on sunny shores,
but that's not what this hotel's for.

Some children travel in a plane,
I can see them flying, if I crane
my neck, standing on window sill,
watch vapour trails hang straight and still.

Some children have a family home
with lots of space where they have grown,
they live behind their own front door,
but that's not what this hotel's for.

TWiNS

The twins are crying,
they're always crying,
the door slams behind me,
makes them cry harder.

Where have you been, all this time?
You're no help, no help at all!
Don't you think I'd like to walk away,
have some space for myself?

The twins are crying.
they're always crying,
I turn and leave, the door slams,
makes them cry harder.

MR AMIR'S GROCERY SHOP

I often end up here,
when I've slammed
the door of
the room
at the hotel.

I never call it
our room,
it's just
the room
at the hotel.

Yes, I often end up here,
chat to Mr Amir
for a while.
He doesn't mind
if I don't buy.

Sometimes,
he gives me jelly beans,
says, *Shh! Don't tell*
the other kids,
it'll be the ruin of me!

RUINED

Nice of you to call in again! shouts Mum.
It's all ruined,
everything's ruined!
I knew that we shouldn't stack
the crockery so high,
but there's just no room,
no room,
no room!

And she's right.

PICKING UP THE PIECES

Mum on her knees,
picking up broken cups,
handles without bodies,
bodies without handles,
nothing fitting together.

I kneel with her,
picking up the pieces,
avoiding the cuts,
careful with the pain –
tears drop between shards.

I tell her, *Never mind,*
picking up on her thoughts
in the space without shouting,
in the space I call room,
filled with sighs and silence.

WAVES

I think back.
The day before Dad left,
he took me to Portsmouth.
The waves crashed against the pier,
again and again, again and again,
a continuous flow of liquid language,
no commas, no full stops.

Not like our conversation.

Silence filled the spaces between each sentence.

Dad was not saying the thing he had meant to say.

I was too scared to ask him to say it.

We watched seagulls and ate chips.

I've not been a very good dad, he said,
but I do love you . . . in my own way.

THE MORNING AFTER

Dad was gone

(I don't want to talk about it)

THEM

BEING FOLLOWED

It's the eyes I can feel,
little pinpricks invading my privacy,
little pinpricks of sight,
like laser beams
fixed on my back
as I walk.

This is the alleyway
I'll take to Spencer's Wood Academy
in September.
Once you've crossed the road that runs
across the middle,
the alleyway leads to the park,
from where you can see the school gates

in the distance,
just the other side of the football pitch,
where, on Sundays, ankles are kicked and
Oi Ref! shoots out of the mouths of
parents watching their prodigies
shooting for the stars.

This will be the hardest part
of my morning walk –

when I can see the gates.
My legs will falter,
my heart will beat faster,
my courage will melt.

I take a deep breath,
swing around,
expecting to see
THEM.
Instead, a little brown dog halts,
stares at my face, turns and leaves.

THEM

It started about 3 months ago,
on my first day at Park Close Primary,
after the move.

Mrs Montgomery led me to the Year 6 classroom
and introduced me to Mr Fellows,
who introduced me to Jess,
who introduced me to Red Table.
I hate introductions,
they always feel awkward,
so I stared at the smoke-grey classroom floor.

I survived until breaktime,
until Jess went to the loo with her friends.
I leant against the playground wall,
wondered what Roxy was doing
at Beavers Brook Primary.

Mr Fellows told us you were coming, on Friday,
shouted a boy with loose, dark curls.
My mum says you live in a hotel, she's seen you!
sneered his freckly friend, with a laugh.
Got any free sugar sachets to share?
The three girls next to them burst into

an exaggerated cackle of giggles.

The whistle sounded, the giggles died,
with my dignity.

HUNTING FOR THE LITTLE BROWN DOG

I stare at the space
that had been filled
with a little brown dog.

I've always liked dogs,
but the flat wasn't big enough,
and we weren't allowed to have one,
anyway.

I retrace my steps, searching behind
every bin parked outside the back gates
of every house, backing onto this alleyway.
I once heard a dustman huffing and puffing
along, collecting bins, moaning,
No bloomin' access to these houses,
you'd think the planners would've thought about that!

I walk out, back along Station Road,
and there he is.

I stare at the space
that has been filled
with a little brown dog.

WAGGING

Wagging is a strange word.
If you're wagging school –
you're in trouble,
if a finger is wagging at you –
you're in trouble,
but when a dog's tail is wagging –
you've got approval.

Good Boy

His coat has been warmed by the sunshine.
I watch the hairs smooth as I stroke down his back,
see them divide between my fingers
as I stroke up towards his head.

I bend towards his face, he licks my cheek.
My eyes search the street for a possible owner,
for a possible home for the little brown dog
who is leaning against my bare shins.

Who's a good boy, then,
who's a good boy,
who's a good boy, then,
who's a good boy . . .

I find a rhythm in my voice, a word song of praise
for his gentle nuzzling, his brown-eyed innocence.
I sit on the curb, he sits, squashes next to me,
unaware that this is the happiest I've felt for ages.

TRACKED DOWN

I make my way back
to the hotel,
brace myself for,
Ava! Where have you been?

I lost sight of
my wagging friend
a few streets ago.

I stand

outside

the door

and

listen.

No crying.

I gently enter
the room.
The twins

are asleep,
Mum is looking
out of the window –
I join her.

I stare at a space
that has been filled
with a little brown dog.

I've been tracked down.

TRACKER

I tell Mum I'll empty our bin
into the big one outside,
(so I can go to see
the little brown dog).

At first, I can't see him –
his conker-brown coat is as dark as the
dusk that is settling
on houses and car bonnets,
on trees and grass.

I listen hard for
a bark
a whimper
a panting.
Nothing.

I search behind the hotel bins,
my fingers skid in slimy egg-white

that

drips

down

the

side

of

one.

Urgh! Yuk! Yuk!

A small brown head pops around the bin,
he wags his tail and

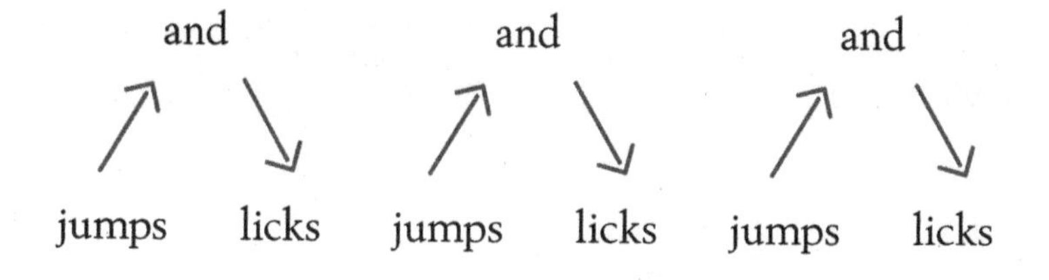

Down boy! Down boy! How did you track me?
Perhaps that's what I should call you!
I stroke his soft head and look into his eyes,
You're Tracker, I shall call you Tracker!

TESCO

This morning
Mum has a mission for me –

If I give you a list,
could you go to Tesco?
They don't deliver
to the likes of us.

I wonder what
'the likes of us' is.

It's a nice morning,
you'll enjoy the outing,
check the sell by dates,
don't bring back mushy fruit.

Mum is right,
it is a nice morning.
Tracker has gone, but
I stroke a cat, strolling
along a wall,
and wave to Mr Amir.

At the entrance to Tesco,
I see THEM,
all 5 of them, together.

I squeeze behind some trolleys,
kneel down, look through the bars
like a prisoner.

LAST DAY OF SCHOOL

On the last day of school, they'd said –

It was just a bit of fun.

We didn't take your stuff, anyway.

You can't take a joke.

Going on holiday anywhere nice?

We know a really cheap hotel.

WE'LL LOOK OUT FOR YOU!

And I knew that they would.

BEHIND BARS

I stay behind bars 'til they swagger away,
'til their backs are dots in the distance.
I've learnt, through the months, it's better to hide,
disappear, run away, no resistance.

I'm good at hiding.
Have been all my life.
Had to hide at
63a, Cromwell Road,
before we moved
to live in
the room.

HIDING UNDER THE STAIRS

They used to hide under the stairs in WW2,
(I read it in a book at Beavers Brook Primary School)
and when the planes had flown over, on to the city,
children would tumble out, legs unfolding like deck
chairs.

We didn't have stairs at Flat 63a, Cromwell Street.
We did have 2 bedrooms, lounge, kitchen, bathroom,
and a cupboard where Mum would make me hide
when Dad returned from the pub, fists clenched.

BOMBS

I remember the evening
Mum told Dad
about the twins.

You stupid cow, should've been more careful.
Is it mine? Bet it isn't. BET. IT. ISN'T!

There . . . there are two of them, Mum replied, softly.

Two of 'em! Where d'you think we can put two?
You did it on purpose, spite, that's what it is.
Get rid, woman. D'you hear, GET RID!

He slammed the front door,
shook the walls,
kicked the recycling box.
His empty beer cans flew up, then
down onto the pavement –
a different kind of clanging shrapnel.

Mrs Taylor, opposite, looked out of her window,
closed her curtains early for the night.

Two hours later, Dad exploded into the flat.

We'd heard him swearing at a distance for ten minutes before the detonation.
Mum said, *Shh! Get in the cupboard, I'll tell him you're at Roxy's. I'll let you know when he's asleep.*

iT WAS BEST NOT TO

It

was

best

not

to

look

through

the

crack

in

the

cupboard

door

EARLY MORNING, AFTER THE EXPLOSION

The morning after the explosion,
Mum woke me early, with a cup of tea.

It's not even 7 o'clock!
I moaned, ungratefully.

I want you out of the flat before your father gets up.
Can you go to Roxy's before school?
By the way,
your father says he's taking you to Portsmouth tomorrow.

I walked along the lane to Roxy's house.
Roxy's mum answered the door.

Come in, love, come in.
Your mum gave me a ring – Roxy's in the kitchen.

I'm sorry it's so early, Mrs Williams.

You have nothing to be sorry about, Ava,
nothing at all.

But I wasn't quite sure she was right.

TWO SCHOOLS

When I started at Park Close Primary,
the term ahead was all the time I had
to make some friends
and some enemies.

But all the friends were taken,
only enemies were looking for
someone new, someone different,
someone like me.

Next term, I'll go to
Spencer's Wood Academy,
but it won't be a fresh start,
just a different uniform.

And every morning,
when I see the school gates,
my eyes will scan the navy jumpers,
until I have THEM in my sights.

SPRAWLING LEGS

The first week of the summer holiday is over.
The dry weather allows me to escape the room.

Today, I sit at the bottom of the slide in the park, alone.
It's probably too early for regular kids to be up.

I think about Roxy – how much I miss her
and her bouncy enthusiasm for . . . everything!

Behind me, a panting turns into a whimper,
I spin around on my bottom, sliding easily on the metal.

Tracker bounds towards me, skinny legs sprawling
into an undignified landing on my bony lap.

I find a rhythm tumbling out of my mouth, again,
rising and falling, rolling over and over,

Who's a good boy, then,
who's a good boy,
who's a good boy, then,
who's a good boy . . .

He settles with me, half on my lap, half on the slide,
and I sing him a song my Nana taught me.

I stroke his limp ears, as he snoozes in the sun,
until the same ears prick up –
he leaps down
and runs.

HEY, AVA

Hey, Ava, over here – it's your lucky day!
Was that your dog? Is your hotel 'dog-friendly'?
He walks over to me, and sits down on the slide.
I can see his black curls out of the corner of my eye.

Hey, Ava, fancy meeting you here today!
shouts another one of them, walking towards me,
sitting on the other side, her long blonde hair hanging
like a curtain between us, such a frail barrier.

Hey, Ava, it's weird you being here with us!
shouts Black Curls' friend, striding towards me,
two giggling girls trailing behind, in tandem.
Not playing with any other friends today?

Well, was that your dog, Ava Booking.com? asks a giggling girl.
(When they'd first called me that, in Mr Fellow's class, I had to google it on Mum's phone, back at the room.)
No, I reply, *he's just a kind of friend.*

All 5 of them burst out laughing, then chorus –

Ava's got a dog friend,
Ava's got a dog friend,
Ava's got a dog friend,
Ava's got a dog friend . . .

This taunting rhythm tumbles out of their mouths,
rising and falling, rolling over and over,

until I start to cry.

MR AMIR'S CHAIR

I pass the shop, on the way home,
and wave to Mr Amir.

He

    sees

the

    tears

falling

    from

my

    brown

eyes

Hey, Ava, he calls, *wait!*

'Hey Ava' from Mr Amir's mouth, sounds gentle – three syllables, full of tender concern.
I marvel at how the same words in different mouths can ride on the same air waves, with so opposite an intention.

I walk over to the shop door.

Are you okay, Ava?

I don't want to talk about it.

How about a ride on my chair – help me with a few customers?

Mr Amir has two tall chairs behind the counter.
My favourite one is the revolving one.
I love that chair.
I love Mr Amir.

THE THING ABOUT THE TWINS

The thing about the twins is
their stuff is everywhere,
makes the place look like a landfill site
full of nappies, cotton wool and stained babygrows.

The thing about the twins is
I have to be quiet when they sleep,
can't even have the telly on low
and walk around in somebody else's world for a while.

The thing about the twins is
they made Dad so angry he left
us behind at 63a, Cromwell Street,
and that was even before they had been born!

The thing about the twins is
they're always in Mum's arms
and in my face, taking my place,
leaving me without any other option than to resent them.

The thing about the twins is
they made us move from the flat,
because without Dad's money, the rent was too much,
so I had to leave Beavers Brook Primary and move to the room.

The thing about the twins is
one has black hair like me and Mum,
the other has sandy-blond hair, reminds me of Dad.
They have names – Noah and Max – but I prefer to say *the twins*.

THE NOTE

I've spent most of the second week of the holiday in the room, hiding.
It's now Friday, and I'm going stir-crazy!

Mum hands me a cup of tea, as I open my eyes.
Some of your friends posted a note under the door this morning, she says.
She hands me a folded piece of A4 lined paper.
I think it's for you, anyway. I opened it because it didn't have a name on.

Hi Booking.com,

It was so nice to see you last week.
Seems like ages since we all had fun
together at school. Why don't we meet
up in the park again on Saturday at 3 p.m.?
If you don't turn up we'll come looking
for you.

See you soon,

Shafiq, Theo, Aleesha, Grace and Lucy

My heart races, I blink away a tear before Mum can see it.

Why do they call you Booking.com, is it an in-joke?

Sort of, I reply, hoping she won't google it.

I'm so relieved you're making friends at last. I know you miss Roxy.

I turn away, walk towards the window, look through prison bars.

NAMES

I did already know their names –
heard them again and again at school,
but I prefer to say *THEM*.

Names are important.
My name means 'bird',
others say it means 'living'.
I googled it at the library.

I think this is ironic.
I don't feel free like a bird,
I don't feel alive,
but it's my name,
one thing that never changes.

Shafiq means 'compassionate',
Theo means 'divine gift',
Aleesha means 'honourable',
Grace means 'kindness and mercy',
Lucy means 'full of light'.
I googled them all.

It's obvious that parents can't predict the future.

THE ESCAPE

THE ESCAPE

I watched a film once where there was a 'safe house'. People were moved there to escape the bad guys.

I thought this was a safe room, but that changed when the note was pushed under the door.

I quietly pack things in Dad's old rucksack – he'd left it at the flat.
Mum wanted to throw it out, but I wanted to keep it.

I take the envelope, full of birthday money from Nana, from the top drawer of the chest by my bed.

(I'm saving it for a bike. We sold my old one. It was tiny. Mum bought us a McDonalds with some of the money.
She was pregnant. She joked, *I can't get any fatter!*
She made lots of jokes – before the twins were born.)

I write a note saying I need to go away for a while.
I tell Mum I love her and I'll come back soon – finish with a big

X

I make sure the door doesn't slam, so the twins don't wake up,
then walk out into the damp, early morning air.
It's 2 a.m.

TIPTOE

The marketplace sleeps quietly.
I tiptoe between the empty wooden stalls,
scared

that

my

footsteps

might

echo

up

to

the

flats

framing

the

small

flagstoned

square.

TARPAULIN

I look up to the night sky, searching for ideas,
searching for the wisdom Nana asks for in prayers.

Looking down again, I untie thin ropes securing tarpaulin over one of the market tables, then tug sharply.

It moves. I slide it off slowly, aware that the dragging sound is amplified in the stillness of this lifeless space.

I quickly fold the tarpaulin into stiff, damp sections, and put the short ropes in the front pocket of the rucksack.

I walk carefully, again, watching an empty carrier bag, blown by the wind, float a soulless haunting around the square.

At the corner of the marketplace, I quicken my steps, then burst into a run, all the way to Spencer's Wood.

SETTING UP CAMP

Mr Amir has tarpaulin over his fruit and veg, just outside the shop.
He's suspended it on poles, and it sits like an awning above the window.

Mr Amir told me –
You can't go wrong with tarpaulin, it's multipurpose.
Tarpaulin is a treasure, keeps out the sun, keeps out the rain.
Marvellous stuff!

And that's what gave me the idea, that's what made me believe I can camp
in Spencer's Wood, near to Spencer's Wood Academy,
if I have a tarpaulin.

And so now I tie it

to four branches over my head

so I can settle

into my warm

sleeping bag

stretch out

my tired legs

rest my head

on my jacket

and sleep.

AS BROWN AS A FOREST FLOOR

I can't feel my legs.
Panic speeds me
into wakefulness.
I rub my eyes,
push my upper body
into a sitting position,
stare at the tree bark
and dry cracked mud
that furnish this
spacious bedroom.

Curled up on my legs,
is a hairy visitor.
He's asleep and
deep in dreams,
nose twitching.
I see that my camp is
just the right place
for a dog as brown
as a forest floor,
for a dog called Tracker.

BIG PAWS

I decide to
snuggle
with Tracker
for a while.
I pull him up
to the top of the
sleeping bag,
until his chin
is on my
shoulder,
his body on
my tummy,
his gangly legs
falling onto
the dry mud
beside me.

He stirs,
looks up,
stares as if
he's watching
his dreams
rush away into
the distance.

Then his head
flops down,
his breath warm
on my neck.
I pick up
a front paw.
It is *so* big,
compared to
his body.

Big paws grow
a big dog!
Nana always says,
so perhaps this
little brown dog
will, one day, be
a big brown dog.

SHREDDIES

I'd packed Shreddies in the rucksack –
not the box, just the inside bag,
but because I have no milk this morning,
we eat them dry – me and Tracker.
He likes Shreddies, although I don't think
they are real Shreddies, just the cheap
Tesco's own variety. We usually had
Tesco's own everything, back at the room,
and at 63a, Cromwell Street. But we never, ever
had Tesco Finest. Suppose it isn't for the likes of us.

I look in my bag, brush off a black beetle and a troop
of ants,
remind myself of what else I'd packed:
biscuits – broken
bread – squashed
peanut butter – nearly empty
half a pack of Doritos – crushed
two apples – only a little bruised
a carton of orange juice – slightly leaking.

Tracker keeps trying to poke his head in the rucksack,
while I check out supplies.

No Tracker, stop it, get your nose out!

He doesn't like my shouting voice.
He lies down, lowers his head onto the mud
between his long front legs, and whimpers.
I jump to my feet, stretch my arms in the air, and yawn.
Tracker backs away, is distressed by my sudden movement,
is wary of my raised arms, as if they signal trouble.

SQUIRREL CHASING

It's Tracker's favourite thing.

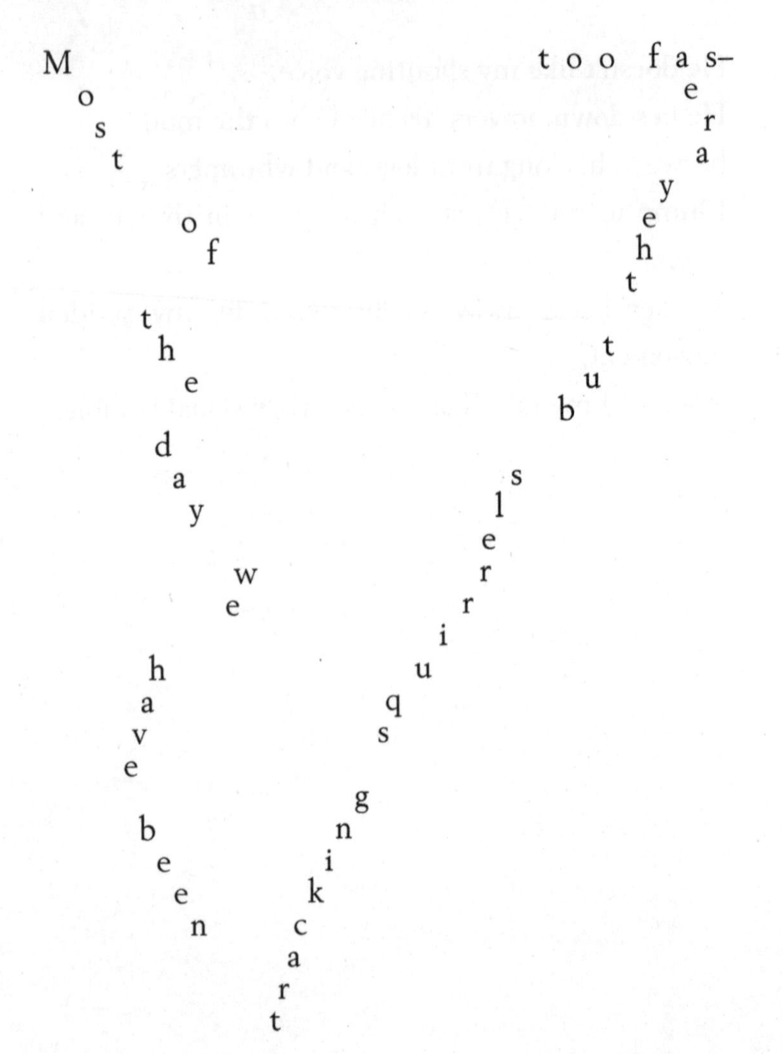

UNDERCOVER

I'm really hungry this evening.
I can smell the fish and chips frying
at Spencer's Road chip shop.
It's not far away from camp,
but I'll have to step out of the woods,
leave the cover of trees and bracken.

I wait

and wait

and wait

to swap the cover of trees for the cover of darkness,
then run, run, run to the chippy, Tracker close at my heels.
Tracker, stay! I say, when I get to the door, and he does.

Bit late for you to be out on your own, says the lady behind the counter.

I'm with my dog – he always protects me.

Well, I hope you're going straight home!

I am, I lie, *2 sausages and chips, please. And ketchup.*

She eyes me suspiciously, through the greasy prongs of her fringe, as she empties chips from her shovel, onto the paper, and tongs the sausages on top, asking, *Salt and vinegar?*
No, thanks, I reply, as I reach over the counter to collect the feast
and pay with a note from Nana's envelope.

We run back to camp, Tracker gets there first, excited by the adventure.
We both sit on my sleeping bag, eat in silence.
Tracker settles down – I stare at the moon, sucking greasy fingers.

DAMP MORNING

Everything is damp –
the sleeping bag
the rucksack
the tarpaulin
Tracker
me.

I feel stiff and cold –
but then Tracker
shuffles up
to my face,
gently
licks.

He nuzzles the rucksack –
sniffing for Shreddies
licking his lips
cocking his
sweet
head.

Sunrays laser through trees –
searching for a girl
and a small dog
in need of
warm
hope.

Beyond the Reach of Hugging

In the middle of the morning,
I hear twigs snapping nearby.

Perhaps others are in the woods –
I think it's Saturday . . . no . . . it's Sunday,

when parents are home and take
their loved children for sunshine walks.

I listen harder, refocus my eyes for
distance viewing, through tunnels of bark.

Voices get louder, then trail off, get lost
in birdsong and forest scampering.

A low growl parts Tracker's agitated lips.
Shh! I say. *Stay! Good boy, good boy.*

One voice soars high above the others –
commanding, firm, yet threaded with anxiety.

Perhaps a loved child has gone missing,
wandered beyond the reach of hugging.

FLORA'S TEA SHOP

I leave the tarpaulin and sleeping bag,
pack everything else, and we leave.
We walk further into the woods,
far away from intruding voices,
until we stumble on a village
with roof-sagging cottages
and smoking chimneys,
and Flora's Tea Shop.
DOG-FRIENDLY
a sign reads, in the tea shop window draped in lace,
and Flora smiles, takes my order for tea,
with toast, and a dog treat.

SIRENS

Police sirens wail through the air,
cut jagged shapes in the atmosphere.

I hate the sound of sirens, Nana often says,
*police, fire engine, ambulance – when it's near,
you always wonder if it's one of your own.*

I watch three police cars race by the tea shop,
lights flashing, briefly reflecting on the milk jug.

More toast? asks Flora. *You can have it for free,
I'm glad of some company when business is slow.
It'll be a different story with the lunchtime rush!
Just made another cup of tea, if you want one.*

And she really does seem to want me to stay.
I accept her offer. Glance at Tracker under the table,
resting, but still locating and eating any stray crumbs.

She pours the tea, and brings it over to my table
with more warm toast – butter melting into pools.

Can you watch for customers? Need to call a supplier.

No problem, glad I can help, I reply cheerfully.

CUSTOMERS

My head is under the gingham-clothed table,
where I'm gently stroking Tracker.
I hear the chiming sound of tinkling bells,
as the tea shop door opens wide.

Two policemen walk in,
approach the counter,
Hello, anyone around?
We got your call!

I straighten up, watch and listen.
Flora appears behind the counter.
She says nothing, just nods towards
where I'm sitting with Tracker.

The policemen both smile at me,
walk slowly to the table, stroke Tracker.
Are you Ava Robertson? says the tall one.
Your mum is beside herself, sighs the other.

They carry my rucksack to their car boot,
place it next to tarpaulin and a sleeping bag,
explain 150 people have been searching
in the woods for me. I slide onto the back seat.

Tracker has to come – HE HAS TO! Tears flow.
He can – for now, smiles the tall policeman,
and Tracker jumps in, sits at my feet,
looking like a very hairy criminal.

I look out of the car window, back towards
the tea shop door, where Flora is standing,
her face darkened by shadows of doubt,
her smile weakened by the guilt of betrayal.

POSTERS

On the back seat, next to me, there are posters.
So many posters – with my photograph on!
I read the text under the photograph –

LOCAL GIRL MISSING – CAN YOU HELP?

A search for missing local girl, Ava Robertson,

will be conducted on Sunday, at 10.30 a.m.,

starting at Spencer's Wood car park.

Ava has been missing since the early hours of Saturday,

and concern for her safety is growing.

All volunteers welcome.

I fold a poster and slip it in my pocket.
I don't know why. Perhaps because I didn't know
so many people would care about the likes of me.

NOAH AND MAX

Where are Noah and Max? I ask,
as Mum rushes towards me
along the corridor at the police station,
sobbing out sound-lumps of fear,
weeping deep pools of relief.
I'm surprised by the feel of
their names in my mouth,
by the syllables of fondness.

They're with Ms Stevens, room 7.
Ms Stevens is the nosiest person
at the hotel – she knows everything.
She has 3 loud children of her own.
I imagine the chaos, the tumbling bodies,
the thudding on the floor, the stress.
We should go and rescue them! I smile,
in an attempt to lighten the mood.

A soft voice floats from the lips of
an officer with gentle eyes, called Beth.
I think we all need to have a chat first.
Perhaps you can help me and your mum
understand what just happened and why.
You're not in trouble, we just want to help.

Words escape from my mouth in a rush –
the move, no space, new school, the bullies . . .

I don't say their names, fearful of revenge,
and Mum can't recall the names on the note.
When you've settled back with Mum, I'll visit,
Beth looks at Mum, *we'll talk about the way ahead.*
What about Tracker? Where is he? He needs me! I cry,
and now tears rush from the burst dam of tension
running through my head, my neck, my back.
The hotel says he can stay tonight, winks Mum.

THiNGS WiLL CHANGE

The familiar smell of my duvet wraps around me.
Tracker curls up at the bottom of my bed,
gently whispers a doggie sigh, buries his head.

The room is quiet, Max and Noah are asleep.
Mum tiptoes over to me and sits, gently.
She brushes wayward curls away from my eyes.

I love you very much. I'm so sorry the twins
gobble up every waking moment, right now –
that will change . . . things will change.

What will happen . . . to . . . Tracker? I ask, falteringly.
He's used to me now – don't think he has an owner.
They're checking, says Mum. A tear slides onto my pillow.

THE BIGGEST WISH

The next morning, Mum wakes me with a cup of tea, as always!
It tastes better than ever before. I hug it to my duvet-covered chest.

You have a busy day ahead, young lady!

Have I?

Yes. Beth from the police station is popping by for a chat this morning, and then . . .

What? What?

You're off to Nana's for a couple of days!

Mum is beaming –
the corners of her mouth almost disappear around the sides of her face!
Mum knows how much I love Nana –
how safe her arms are,
how wise her words sound,
how deep her love is.

How will I get there?

Mr Amir is going to drive you, and pick you up again on Wednesday evening.

I eat breakfast, feed Tracker some Shreddies.

But what about Tracker?

If the police don't find his owner, he can go with you, Nana is allowed pets.

I wish the biggest wish of my entire life.

A WiSH COME TRUE

Beth arrives at 11 a.m., with the same soft voice and gentle eyes.
Some people stay the same person, day after day.
Dad is two people – I like one, I don't like the other.

Beth suggests she and Mum take the twins around the block in the buggy,
so they can talk about grown-up things. She says I'd find it boring.

Mum says, *You stay here and look after Tracker, we won't be very long.*

And they aren't.

Beth asks lots of questions, and I try to answer the best I can.
I don't know the answer to some of the questions, but she doesn't mind.
This goes on for a while, until we reach the moment I've been waiting for.

Is there anything you want to ask me, Ava?

Yes, yes, it's really important! Have you found Tracker's owner?

Well, no, actually, we don't seem to be able to. Nobody has reported him missing.
I punch the air again and again, tickle Max, ruffle Noah's tufty hair, hug Mum.

Can he come to Nana's then, Mum, can he come to Nana's?

Yes, he can! But we need to talk about Tracker when you get back. We can't have pets.

Beth glances at Mum, and their eyes lock, as if the same thought is suspended
between them, as if they have decided words are not a good idea right now.

I sit and wonder if an EVEN BIGGER WISH, would seem like greed.

LITTLE LIGHT

MR AMIR'S DELIVERY VAN

The ancient delivery van is green.
AMIR'S GROCERY SHOP is on the side.
There are just two seats in the front,
so Tracker has to sit on the floor.

I watch as the houses pass by
on familiar streets I know well.
We turn left at the park, travel on
to the straight lines of the M3.

The rhythms of travel vibrate,
play on my back, tickle my ears.
I guess the age of Mr Amir's van –
I think the answer is VERY old.

Sorry if there's a smell of veg, Ava,
says Mr Amir, with a wide smile.
When you arrive at your Nana's house
you might smell like a cabbage!

We both burst out laughing.
Nana really won't mind, I reply.
Maybe not, he chuckles , *but she might*
run you a hot bath! Giggling continues.

THE SIGNS WERE THERE

Signs for Southampton
signs to the Tesco Extra
Cromwell Street road sign.

Signs to Beavers Brook
signs to the children's centre
signs to the dock yards.

Significant signs
that signal previous life,
familiar sights.

We pass every sign
until we see Nana wave
her soft breeze of hope.

TRACKER GETS A TREAT

Nana makes a cup of tea
(Mr Amir brought cakes),
everyone makes a fuss of Tracker,
and Nana gives him a drink.

She opens the back door
and Tracker dashes out,
zooms around the garden
lap after lap after lap.

Must be a real treat,
says Mr Amir, sipping tea,
having such a big garden.
My yard is full of baked beans!

The three of us giggle together,
watch Tracker through the window
sniffing, jumping, rolling, running,
marking his new territory.

SMELLS

Nana has made her famous meat pie.
I could smell it cooking in the oven,
when Mr Amir was still here.

She dishes it up with mash and veg.
I watch the gravy run down the mound
of mash, and flood the peas and carrots.

All the smells are here, at Nana's –
aromas of safety, the fragrance of love.
I breathe in deeply, hold my breath.

I know that soon she will say, *Bath time!*
so I finish eating and go up to the bedroom.
On my bed, I can see a new pair of pyjamas.

The clinking of washing up climbs the stairs,
mingles with the sound of a running bath.
Droplets of happiness fill my wide eyes.

QUIET SITTING

Downstairs, Nana sits next to me, her sofa is a bit saggy.
Read me a story, Nana, The Magic Faraway Tree.
I've put it by your bed for later, for now let's sit
without noise, and without talking, just rest.
Tracker joins in, he's very good at resting.
Why do we have to be quiet, it's weird!
Ava, your head is full of lots of noise,
you need to escape for a while,
let your thoughts untangle
so you can hear them
one at a time, until
they trail off into
quiet sitting.

Everything is still.
Quiet sitting
works.

THE MAGIC FARAWAY TREE

The cover of *The Magic Faraway Tree* is tatty –
it was Nana's book when she was a girl.

Nana often reads it to me when I stay –
I don't care if I'm getting too old for it.

I'm lying still in bed, listening to her.
I imagine sliding down the slippery slip.

The moon shadows on the bedroom ceiling,
adopt their familiar places and shapes.

I want to find out what magical land is
waiting at the top of the towering tree,

but my eyelids keep meeting together,
and the sound of her voice grows faint.

My thoughts start to fade at the edges,
I slide down the slippery slip of sleep.

EARLY MORNING SUN

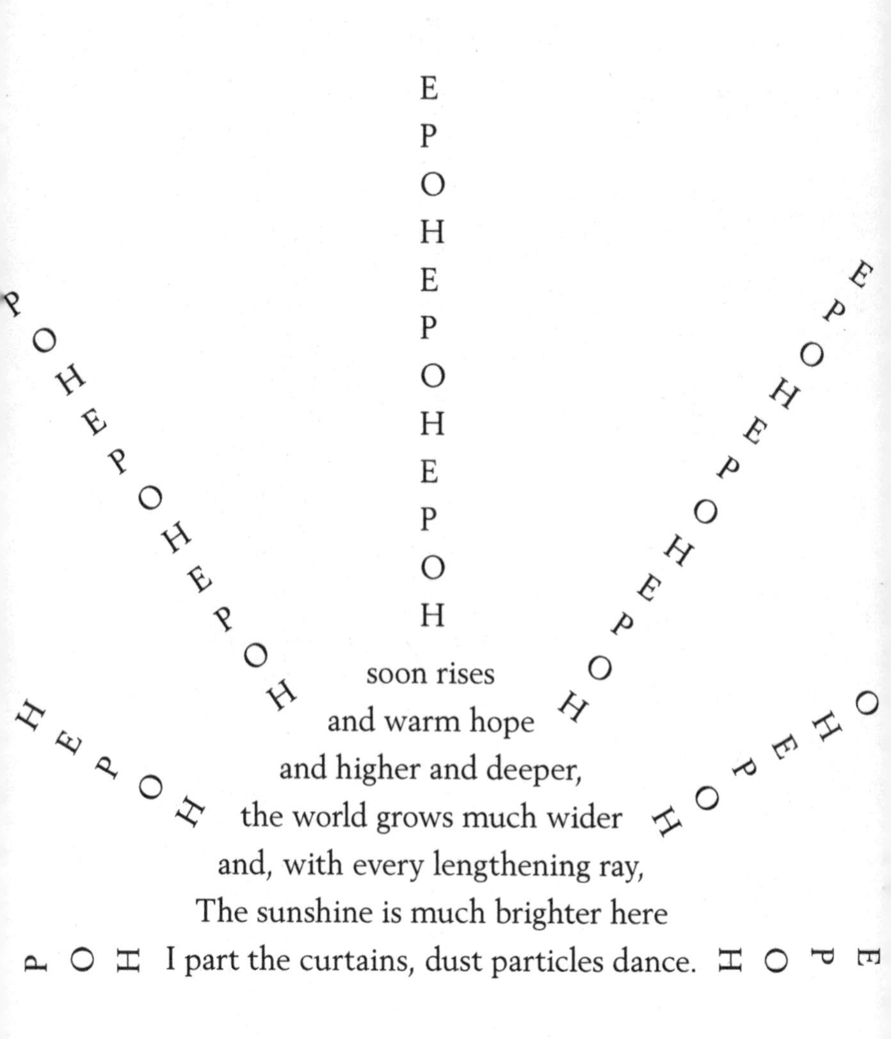

soon rises
and warm hope
and higher and deeper,
the world grows much wider
and, with every lengthening ray,
The sunshine is much brighter here
I part the curtains, dust particles dance.

LiST

Make a wish list, says Nana,
as we sit eating pancakes with maple syrup,
write down what you'd like to do today.

So I do and I make it rhyme
to make it sound as happy as I feel!

WiSH LiST

A bus ride to town
A walk round the shops
A look in the joke store
at all of the props
A play in the park
A walk in the stream
Lunch at the tea shop
(the one by the green)
Get a collar for Tracker
and a lead to attach
for taking him walking
(I'd like them to match)
A bowl for his water
A food bowl to fill
and a blanket to lie on
when he sleeps or is ill.

I think that's all.

Nana let me do it all, and we went to the library.

THAT DOG'S TAKEN A SHINE TO YOU

On Wednesday, we go for a long walk.
Tracker doesn't like his lead.
He keeps sitting down and won't budge, in protest.

He's used to being free, says Nana, *he'll take some training.*
She ruffles his hair, looks in his eyes, he licks her nose.

It's good to be free, Ava, it's like we're made for it,
but not if it leads to danger,
like when you went camping alone in the woods.

That's the only thing Nana has said
about what happened.
She has a gift for saying wise things without a fuss.

Tracker sees another dog in the distance
and he's off like a rocket.
I hold on tight to the lead, trip and fall with a thud.

Tracker stops, turns and nuzzles my head,
sits quietly, whimpers in my ear.
That dog's taken a shine to you, says Nana, grinning.

LITTLE LIGHT

Nana makes jerk chicken for tea.
She always makes sure it's not too hot and spicy for me.
Tell me that story again, Nana, I plead,
the one about when your Nana Anya gave you hot chicken, when you stayed with her in Trinidad!

Oh my, Ava, don't you get tired of that story! she laughs.

But she tells me the story, with all the wild actions, desperately fanning her open mouth with her hands, reaching for water, running around in circles, screaming!

But when we eat, everything is still,
because we both know
that I'm going home this evening.

Nana, I wish I could stay longer,
there's so much light in your house.
Where we live there's too much darkness.

Nana starts to sing our song –

This little light of mine
I'm gonna let it shine
Oh, this little light of mine
I'm gonna let it shine

I join in.

This little light of mine
I'm gonna let it shine
Let it shine
Let it shine
Let it shine.

Nana suddenly flicks the light off and strikes a match.
See how bright one match can be in a dark place, Ava?
She blows out the match and turns the light back on.
You can choose to shine light, Ava, I've told you that,
you just need to be brave enough to shine it.

THE NORTH STAR

SiLENCE

Mum is standing by the front door of the hotel.
I say a cheery goodbye to Mr Amir,
although I don't feel cheery.

Thank you, so much! Mum calls to him.
It's my pleasure – your mum is a lovely lady!
he calls back from the lowered van window.

Where are Noah and Max? I ask.
Asleep – Ms Stevens is watching them again.
Mum hugs me close, Tracker jumps up to join in.

Wow! I've not noticed how big Tracker is getting!
I bet he enjoyed Nana's garden.
I see he's got a collar and lead – did you take him for walks?

I tell Mum all about Tracker's protests.
He's used to it now. As soon as I pick it up
he wags his tail like a high-speed windscreen wiper!

Nana thinks he's an Irish Setter.
She showed me pictures. Oh boy, they're big!
I love him so much, Mum.

Silence.

Let's get you both up to the room.
I want to hear all about what you did with Nana.
I've missed you so much, Ava!

SERIOUS THINKING

The next day we stay in our pyjamas for a while, enjoying a relaxed morning. Even Noah and Max play happily!
But then she says it.

Tracker will need lots of room, she sighs, as she strokes his long back.

STOP IT!
STOP IT!
STOP IT!

I DON'T WANT YOU TO SAY IT!

IT'S NOT FAIR!
IT'S NOT FAIR!

Mum hangs her head.

I get dressed and pick up Tracker's lead. His tail wags furiously.

I need to take him out – he'll be bursting for a wee!

Okay, Mum says, as I'm disappearing out of the door.
Don't be too long, Beth is calling by at lunchtime.

I walk my not-so-little brown dog along local streets.
He sniffs and wags, sniffs and wags – tracking a trail.

I need to do some serious thinking.

THE NORTH STAR

There's a car park next to the hotel,
between us and The North Star pub.
The pub is closed for refurbishments –
it's been closed for ages and ages!

As we pass by, Tracker stops to sniff
the temporary fence surrounding it.
I peep through the gap between panels,
notice the destruction of trespassers.

My tiny buds of serious thinking
blossom into flowers of inspiration.
If trespassers have been in there,
there must be a way in for others,

others like me, who urgently need
to find a home for a not-so-little dog,
a home that is very near to a hotel
where you're not allowed to have pets.

TRESPASSERS

Tracker
wriggles
through
a gap,

I follow,
get stuck,
snagged
on wire,

my jumper
sleeve has
been speared,
I'm captured,

I tug hard,
wool threads
stretch and
pull apart

I'm free to
follow after
Tracker,
behind the

DANGER
KEEP OUT
PRIVATE
signage,

through
the badly
vandalised
front door,

free to
trespass
in The
North Star.

STiCKY

The soles of my feet
stick to the planks
where drinkers got
drunk, and drunks got
sent home to bed.

I trace rings left from
glasses with my finger –
feel the tacky pull
attach my fingertip
to the dark oak bar.

Drink had a tacky pull
for Dad, made sure he
got stuck, time and again.
I wonder where he is now,
which pub he's stuck in.

heart.
my
as
fast
as
flutter
wings
their

pigeons,
at startled
Tracker rushes
stairs.
the
up
We tiptoe

to Tracker
Stay!
whisper
rigid,
I stand
upstairs.
There's a noise

FLUTTER

PERFECT

When we left 63a, Cromwell Road,
we had to fill in an inventory.
It's a list of things in a property.

Downstairs, in The North Star, there are –

Two huge blue sofas, covered with dust sheets.
Drawn curtains, keeping out light, threadbare and torn.
A wide screen TV, unplugged, cracked and dented.
A swinging patio door, prised open by the fingers of a wind gust.
A walled garden with a wooden gate, tightly locked in place.

The perfect hideout for Tracker.

OSCAR

I stand outside the room, listen to the voices, Beth is there.
I revisit a sad memory, squeeze out as many tears as possible,
then storm into the room, uttering noises of deep despair,
swinging the empty collar hanging from the matching lead.

Ava! Ava! Where's Tracker? What's happened? Where is he?
Mum's voice is edged with hysteria and complete disbelief.
Beth's voice pours healing oil on the chaos and confusion,
Take your time, Ava, she says, *tell us exactly what happened.*

I lie well, have worked myself up into a frenzy of grief and regret.
How did he slip his collar? Mum asks. *Wasn't it tight enough?*
I decide it's best to wail loudly to discourage further questions.
Interrogation dissolves into sympathy and hugs. I deserve an Oscar!

GETTING SUPPLIES

After lunch, when Beth has gone, Mum says she needs the loo.
This is the moment I've been waiting for, but I need to be quick.

I fold into Tracker's cosy blanket his lead, collar and food bowls,
shout through the door to Mum, *I'm going to search for Tracker!*

Okay, make sure you're back here for 5, Nana's going to phone us!
She'll be very sad about Tracker. My cheeks redden with deception.

I slip out the door, relieved that Max and Noah have yet to develop
enough language skills to drop a sibling in it up to her neck!

Near the end of Moor Road, there's a pet shop called 'The Paw Store'.
I place the blanket on the floor. The bowls clunk. I open an envelope.

Nana's birthday money gift is nearly all gone, but I have enough.
I'd like a medium bag of dried dog food, please, I tell the lady.

New dog? she asks. *How old? What size is it? Any dietary needs?*
I answer as well as I can – wonder why life is full of interrogations.

THE LIKES OF ME

Safe in The North Star –
if I could stay, too, we'd be
the perfect housemates.

But it's nearly 5,
time for Nana to phone us –
speak petal-soft love.

I will dream sweet dreams
knowing that Tracker is near,
dreaming sweet dog dreams.

Good boy, stay! Good boy!
I say as I slide out to the bar
then through the front door.

And deep in my heart
I know this place is a gift
to the likes of me.

HOME IS WHERE THE HEART IS

A
home
is where your
heart is, so they say.
Mine's here at The North Star
where I've set up home for Tracker –
his blanket on a sofa, bowls by the patio door.
He has a garden to roam in, water from a water butt.
All his worldly wealth is under one roof,
and my worldly wealth is here, too –
waiting for me to walk in for cuddles,
for breakfast, waiting for, *Good Boy!*
He hears the front door push open,
jumps, scratching at the lounge door,
then dances his frenzy of welcome
as I open it, kneel down to hug him.
He licks my face clean of night's grip.

I TELL MUM

I tell Mum I think I've seen Tracker
in Spencer's Road . . . near the chip shop.
Adding that detail was better lying.

I tell Mum, *On the way back I met some*
friends in the park, we had loads of fun.
Her smile almost makes me feel guilty.

I tell Mum I stopped to chat to Mr Amir.
I'm sorry I've been so long. What's for tea?
I'm starving, it's all the fresh air, I suppose.

I tell Mum everything

but the truth.

MiNE

A couple of days go by and I
get used to a routine with Tracker.

A couple of nights go by and I
get used to him being safe.

A couple of weeks go by and I
get used to him being mine.

SECRETS

ROXY IS COMING TO STAY

This is a beautiful morning,
this is a wonderful day,
the sun warms my face by the window
and Roxy is coming to stay.

I look at the road just below us,
the cars shine in every bay,
I notice that Noah and Max are quite cute,
now Roxy is coming to stay.

Mum makes a joke and I laugh
in a slightly hysterical way,
I wave to Ms Stevens, as she passes by
because Roxy is coming to stay.

Her mum says that it'll be fine
and just one night will be okay,
so we'll sleep top to tail in my single bed,
make room so that Roxy can stay.

SHARING SECRETS

Mrs Williams drops Roxy off at 8.30 a.m.
There is so much giggling to be done!

Roxy shares some secrets I can't tell you,
about teachers back at Beavers Brook Primary.

When she's finished, I tell her we'll go to the park,
Can we take a sandwich, Mum, have a picnic?

Mum thinks it's a great idea, makes cheese sandwiches,
puts them in a carrier bag with bananas and Kit Kats.

Make the most of the day, she says, *don't hurry,*
show Roxy the sights, introduce her to some friends.

I feel very excited, as we walk out of the door.
I've been bursting to tell my secret, the best secret.

How far is the park, Ava? asks Roxy as we walk.
We're not going to the park, I reply, with a wink.

Are we going to meet some of your new friends?
I look down. *Don't have any new friends, apart from one.*

Roxy frowns. *So are you going to show me the sights?*
I'll show you the only sight worth seeing, I say, *just here.*

Bouncy Little Giggles

Where? Where's this amazing sight? asks Roxy.
Right here, I say, pointing to The North Star.

Have you gone crazy? It's ugly . . . it's all smashed up!

Some ugly things are beautiful inside, you'll see.

Roxy follows me round to the gap in the fence.
What are you doing? You can't go in there!

I go in here every day, I keep my secret here.

Roxy's eyes open wide. *You really mean it, don't you?*
Just follow me, squeeze through the gap here, I instruct.

Roxy's fear breaks into bouncy little giggles.
By the time we push through the tatty front door,
she's doubled up with laughter, tears streaming.
She holds on to the oak bar, trying to straighten up,
attempting to catch her breath so she can talk.

Urgh! It's so sticky! This place is gross! she cries.

And then she hears . . . *the scratching.*

3 OUT OF 4

It's too dangerous to go in,
says Roxy.
There's something in there,
says Roxy.
Bet it's hairy with big teeth,
says Roxy.
It'll jump us on the other side,
says Roxy.

It's not dangerous to go in,
I say,
but you've scored 3 out of 4!

ZOOOOM!

Roxy holds her breath, clings to my arm
as I open the creaky door very slowly.
First, a paw stretches out, a black nose sniffs,
then *ZOOOOM!* a brown dog shoots
through

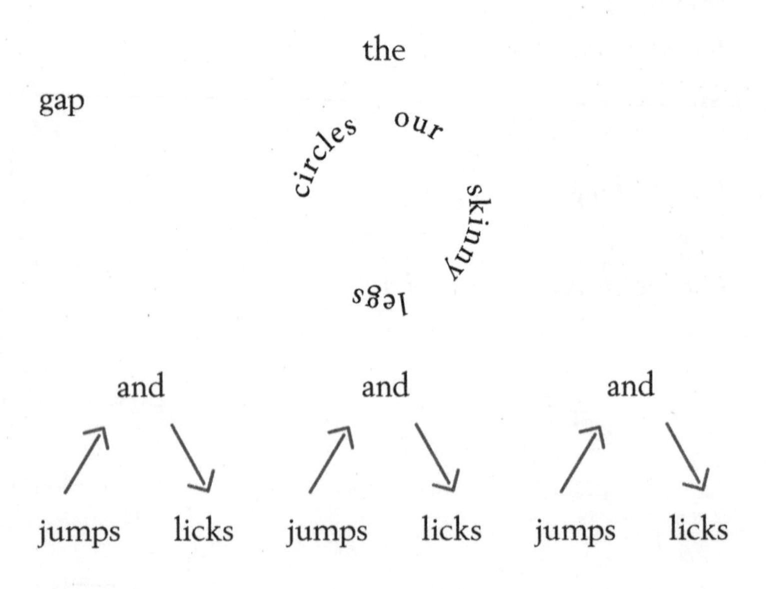

then rolls on his back, legs stretching out like gangly tree branches.

This is my friend Tracker! I gush, falling to my knees for a cuddle.

THE WHOLE TRUTH, AND NOTHING BUT THE TRUTH

I tell Roxy the story of Tracker, the truth, the whole truth,
and nothing but the truth, even about the bullies in the park.

So, if the water's cut off, how do you get water for him? Roxy asks, when I've reached the happy ending of the story.

I beckon her through the patio doors, Tracker follows.
I take her to the water butt at the end of the walled garden.

Look, there's a tap at the bottom. I demonstrate with pride.
I fill his bowl here twice a day, when I feed him. Tracker sniffs it.

This is AMAZING! enthuses Roxy, quickly trying the tap.
You've got everything so organised. It's the best secret ***ever****!*

Tracker nuzzles her face while she's bent over at the tap,
until she collapses onto her bottom, shouting, *TRACKER!*

We sit on the grass, in the sun, and Tracker stretches out.
As time goes by he starts to pant but enjoys the searing heat!

In the garden there are 5 pub picnic benches, 3 are broken.
We move to one to eat our lunch, even though it's only 11 a.m.

The barky arms of a huge tree, cover us with a cloak of shade –
a magic cloak, covered with stars of secrecy and friendship.

Roxy&Me.com

We laze on dusty sofas,
chat about old times.
One subject leads to another,
no effort, no pressure.
It's always been like this,
Roxy&Me.com

We met in Year 3,
immediately knew that
our thoughts merged,
that one look said enough
in our secret language,
Roxy&Me.com

Tracker sniffs his lead,
glances at me, then Roxy.
Her blue eyes meet my brown.
It'll be a bit risky, we chorus,
laughing at our unity,
Roxy&Me.com

RUNNING FREE

We
squeeze
through
the
fence,

turn the opposite way to the hotel,

down past Bill's Scrapyard,

along Bridge Street

to the big green, where Tracker can

r

u

n

f e

r e

DOUBLING BACK

I'd intended to take Roxy along by the river but,
across the other side of the green, I can see
a boy with black curly hair, another boy who,
I'm sure, has a freckly face, and three girls.

What's wrong? asks Roxy. *D'you know them?*
Our eyes meet. *Booking.com* is all I need to say.
We'll go back the way we came, I blurt out.
I turn and walk quickly, as Roxy calls Tracker.

My heart thumps wildly, until we're past
Bill's Scrapyard and are safely back home.
We collapse onto a sofa, Tracker laps up water.
In the silence, I can hear birds singing in the garden.

You can't live like this forever, Roxy sighs,
you're good at hiding, always have been,
but sometimes you have to step outside.
I knew she wasn't talking about The North Star.

SHOWING OFF

We shut Tracker in, after we've given him dinner,
and leave him for the night. He's such a good boy.

Hope you've had a really lovely day, says Mum,
as she waves packs of microwave meals in the air.

Which one do you fancy? she asks Roxy, with a sigh.
We only use our microwave, don't use the kitchen much.

Mum is right, only two hotel families use the kitchen,
they think it's their own, don't like to have visitors.

The sausage and mash one, please, answers Roxy.
Got cheesecake, too! beams Mum, raising the tone.

We eat on our laps and tell Mum all about our day.
We tell a bit of the truth, definitely not the whole
truth.

Noah and Max make bread pellets, roll them,
throw them, their hands sticky with baked beans.

The cheesecake isn't Tesco's own, it's Tesco Finest.
Mum is showing off because Roxy is staying tonight.

TICKLISH TOES

We don't sleep well,
Roxy has ticklish toes.
Each time our bodies touch,
she jerks her legs away.

After breakfast, we walk
to The North Star,
enter super quietly
to catch Tracker snoozing.

I push my finger into
a paw pad of toes,
Tracker has ticklish toes,
he jerks his leg away.

And then we all dance,
celebrating ticklishness
and mornings and the
tolerance of real friends.

THE CHANGING OF THE LIGHT

It's now 4 o'clock,
and soon we will lock
Tracker in here for the night.

Shadows are longer
my feelings get stronger
with the changing of the light.

The day has been fun
and we let Tracker run
on the green without bullies in sight.

And we talk of the past
but the time goes so fast,
like a peregrine falcon in flight.

And the tick and the tock
fill my head with the knock
of real life, which makes me uptight.

Then straight after tea
we'll look out 'til we see
Mrs Williams' car, shiny and bright.

Then Roxy will go,
and my heart will sink low,
having soared from a magical height.

AN HOUR LATER

Roxy was gone

(I don't want to talk about it)

THE GAP

The summer holiday is getting shorter
as days disappear, transfer to the past,
leaving less of a gap, less hiding space
between me and Spencer's Wood school.

I explain this all to Tracker, at breakfast,
in The North Star, before I go back to
the room, before I let Mum take me to
town, to buy my new school uniform.

I will look the part – look the same as
children who live in houses with kitchens
that they're allowed to use at any time,
houses where they're allowed to have pets.

And then, I will just count the days
before my classmates start to see
how wide the gap is between us –
the likes of them and the likes of me.

BRIDGING . . .

Monday morning, the shoe shops are full
of small feet that have got bigger
over the long summer break.
Bags of pencil cases
and new uniforms
swing in time to
the rhythm
of new
starts

. . . THE GAP

Monday afternoon, my bags are full
of Spencer's Wood Academy.
Between the handles I see
the flood of navy-blue,
the tide is changing.
Go with the flow,
Mum will say,
take deep
breaths

A VISIT FROM NANA

On Tuesday Nana comes to visit us,
she caught the 9.15, which doesn't stop
until it reaches Eastleigh's railway station,
she steps down from the train at 10 o'clock.
She hands me new school trainers in a box,
and gives the shop receipt to Mum to keep,
she holds my hand as we walk along the path,
the twins are in the buggy, fast asleep.
She says, *Let's go to Costa for a coffee*
(I have a chocolate muffin with some tea)
and we sit around the table for a chat
Nana and Mum, the twins (asleep) and me.
        The world around is silent as we sit,
        as if we five are set apart from it.

ANOTHER WALK WITH NANA

So, where is he? Nana asks, when we leave the hotel for air.
A walk is not the same without a dog, she says with a wink.

Uh, what do you mean? I ask, my innocent eyes wide open,
uncertain of her meaning, hesitant in my speaking.

Ava, you can't fool me the way you can fool others.
Where's Tracker? I'd love to see how big he's grown.

I get a fit of the giggles, Nana catches them from me.
He's in The North Star, just across the car park, I confess.

I point my finger at the pub. She rolls her eyes, shakes her head.
We walk to the fence, past
DANGER – KEEP OUT – PRIVATE.

And then she s t r e t c h e s the fence a little wider,
follows me through the door, the bar and into the lounge.

Tracker leaps at Nana, chases in a circle around her legs, bounds from one sofa to the other, and back again.

Tracker! Tracker! I shout. *Calm down, calm down.*
He's fine, insists Nana, *he's just pleased to see me.*

I show Nana the garden, the water butt, the benches.
Young Tracker has more room than you! she laughs.

Will . . . you . . . tell Mum? I ask, miserably.
Nana looks into my eyes,
I'll have to have a good think about it, she sighs, *it's tricky.*

We sit in the garden and listen to the birds singing. No need to say anything when you're doing quiet sitting.

Passing on a Secret

Mum knows my secret,
Nana passed it to her wrapped
in wise words and love.

When she opened it,
she looked at Nana, then me.
We'll share him, she said.

And grey clouds parted,
cut through by bright, sharp sunrays,
distant birds sang hope.

THE LAST WEEK

During the last week of the holiday,
Mum visits Tracker with me each day.
I have to pass the twins through the fence.

Mum thinks the building is old but safe,
but it's best to stay downstairs. She jokes,
It's like the houses on Homes Under the Hammer*!*

Today, the four of us sit at a picnic bench,
to eat ham rolls, Quavers and sweet, shiny apples,
and I wish this day could go on and on, that it could
be **now** forever.

SPENCER'S WOOD ACADEMY

FIRES

The day before school starts,
Mum says she has BIG NEWS.
With crossed fingers, I ask,
Has the school burnt down?

Mum frowns, stares at me.
You really shouldn't say that.
Fires are dangerous, fires kill,
you should never wish for one!

I know, I agree, *I'm just anxious*
about walking there, being there.
I don't even have any friends
to walk with, to be nervous with.

Mum strokes my fringe back, gently.
I'll walk with you, with the twins.
No, no, please don't do that, I beg,
that will make things worse for me.

I imagine THEM, watching me
walk with my mum. Imagine their
sparks of hot spite join to build
a huge bonfire of raging scorn.

BIG NEWS

I ask Mum to tell me the BIG NEWS.
Beth called. She's talked to the council.
We're moving into a house in 2 weeks.

Back home? Are we going home? I yell.

No, Ava, we're moving nearer to your school,
just around the corner, in fact, on the edge
of Swallow's Rest village – you've been there.

Where Flora's Tea Shop is? I ask her. She nods.

We're being moved to Spencer's Estate,
so we won't be in the village, itself.
It's 5 minutes' walk from the Academy.

We'll have 3 bedrooms, lounge, kitchen, bathroom
and a big back garden, with 2 apple trees.
Beth says we're getting some furniture, too.

YES! YES! YES!

I bounce on my bed and punch the air.
Then I stop. We'll be a long way from

The North Star – from Tracker.

I sit quietly and try to take everything in.
I hold each thought, turn it around slowly,
look at each one until I can see it properly.

It's okay, Ava, don't worry – he can come, too.

YES! YES! YES!

MR AMIR'S POEM

After tea, Mum asks me to get milk.
I smile my way to Amir's Grocery Shop,
dancing from one flagstone to another.

I tell Mr Amir the BIG NEWS, and he claps.
Ava, that's such good news, I'm so happy!
I'll miss you, though, please come to see me.

Mr Amir gives me a huge hug – I hug back.
We don't go for another two weeks, I sigh,
I have to start at Spencer's Wood Academy first.

You sound sad now, Ava, what's wrong?
I tell Mr Amir about the bullies, about my fear.
Look out for customers, Ava, I have a job to do.

A few minutes later, Mr Amir returns.
This is for you to take to school, he whispers,
it will keep you company, it will be your friend.

He hands me a folded piece of paper. I open it.

There was a young lady called Ava,
Who loved every jelly bean flavour.
She took some to school,
Made the other kids drool –
What terribly shocking behaviour!

We laugh together, until I know I should get back. I pick up the milk and turn to go. *Don't forget these!* calls Mr Amir, handing me a jumbo bag of jelly beans.

Walking to School

Morning
prods me awake.
I dress before breakfast,
so I know I'm ready to go.
Deep breath.

The street
(full of children
wearing squeaky clean shoes)
flows like a navy-blue river.
I swim.

I stop
for a moment,
to pull up my white socks
crumpled at my skinny ankles.
Stand straight.

I pick
up my pace now,
keep going, keep going,
go with the flow down the alley.
For now.

The gates
swallow me up.
I stare down at my feet,
pull my hood down over my eyes.
I hide.

ASSEMBLY

we file in,
one long,
snaking line,
stand at
the front
and sit on
command,
quietly.

we listen
we sing,
my heart
lifts a little,
the girl
next to me
turns to
smile,

but when
we file out,
a leg bars
my way
I trip and
I slip and

I fall and
I blush.

CLASS MIRACLE 1

It's a miracle –
Shafiq is in Class T1
It's a miracle –
Theo and Aleesha are in Class K1
It's a miracle –
Grace and Lucy are in Class W1
It's a miracle –
I'm in Class M1
Class Miracle 1!
(Nana must have prayed.)

Precious

At morning break, I hide
with a girl called Precious.
She doesn't have a pack of friends, either,
she doesn't feel precious at school.

We sit in a playground corner, with our hoods up,
even though the September breeze
is gentle on our faces,
even though the autumn sun
warms our shoulders.

I slip her some jelly beans,
quietly defying a school rule, 'No Sweets'.
I'm good at quiet defiance –
defiance that nobody notices
unless you're careless,
unless you bring attention to yourself.

I never bring attention to myself,
it always leads to trouble –
much better to hide under a market table,

in a cupboard, in a pub, a playground corner.
Precious likes the green and red jelly beans.
I love them all but my favourites are orange and black.
We're a match made in Heaven!

Then, a chant erects a fence around us –
Booking.com! Booking.com! Booking.com!
I refuse to look at their faces, and block my ears.
Precious puts an arm around my shoulders.
We turn away, stare at the two walls that meet behind us, walls that trap us and protect us,
until the whistle blows, and spite is stilled to silence.
Silence walks with us, back to the classroom.

A HOUSE LIKE ROXY'S

After school, we pick up Precious' phone from Reception, phone Mum to ask if I can hang out at Precious' house.

Ava, you've made a new friend on the very first day!
Of course you can hang out, just be back by 6 for tea.

Mum is so excited, it makes me laugh. I imitate her voice, make Precious laugh at my over-the-top squealing.

Precious lives on Spencer's Estate. I tell her I'm moving there.
We try to guess which empty house will be mine, as we walk.

I thought her house would be big and posh, just like Roxy's, but it's not. It's more ordinary, it's more worn and repaired.

Her mum pops her head around the door. *Welcome, Ava, Precious texted me about you!* She's got a Mrs Williams smile.

Precious shows me some of the clothes in her wardrobe, she has a bedroom all to herself. Her brother's is next door.

Do you have a dad? I ask. She hands me a photo in a frame.
I have two, but this one lives in another country. Do you?

Doesn't feel like it. Don't know where my dad lives now. And we leave it at that. Play games on Precious' phone.

We hear the front door open, and soon I meet Precious' dad.
He asks how school went, asks if we're hungry, says, *I've got cakes!*

He tells some jokes as bad as the ones Mr Williams tells.
I groan loudly, along with Precious and her mum.

I leave at 5.30, walk to the hotel, tell Mum about Precious,
about how her house isn't posh, but is just like Roxy's.

WET PLAY

i w t d f b

t' e h r o e

s t e o r t

w p d p m w

e l a s b e

d a y d a e

n y a r r n

e s s i r tl

s a r p i kl

d v a a e wl

a e i n r &

y s n d s ml

A RAINY WEEK AHEAD

The weather girl says
the rain will last 'til Saturday.
Sunbeams fill my heart.

SATURDAY

It's Saturday,
I've survived one whole week of school.
Mum says,
After breakfast, we must start packing.

Last Saturday,
we watched the people in room 19 moving out.
Mum said,
Those boxes don't look very sturdy to me.

Next Saturday,
we'll be moving to Spencer's Estate!
Mum says,
Mr Amir's going to bring us some strong boxes.

One Saturday,
we saw a big removals van outside a house.
Mum said,
We don't have enough stuff to fill that cab!

Saturday coming,
we'll shut the door of the room, forevermore.
Mum says,
We'll turn a page, we'll finish a chapter.

I hope the book gets better.

SUNDAY

Sunday fades quickly into Monday

HIDING IN THE LIBRARY

I'm hiding in the library with Precious.
We saw a poster asking for librarians.
Mrs Reynolds is going to train us both –
she's started us off on book covering.

The school library has been refurbished –
it's a selling point displayed on open days.
We can even eat our lunch in the office
Mon-Fri, as there are only three volunteers.

I like books – I hide between the covers.
You can watch what other people do
without them knowing you're there.
They never ask, *What are you staring at?*

Mrs Reynolds says we can borrow books,
as many books as we want to, cos we help.
That means I can take hundreds of people
home, when I move to 14, Woodcutter's Road.

If **they** come into the library, we can stand
behind the counter – they're not allowed to.
In the library, they can't write my story,
I'm in charge of the characters and the plot.

JELLY BEAN MYSTERY

We've helped Mrs Reynolds all week.
She has a supply of jelly beans for helpers.

I tell her and Precious about Mr Amir.
I read them his poem – I always take it to school.

There was a young lady called Ava,
Who loved every jelly bean flavour.
She took some to school,
Made the other kids drool –
What terribly shocking behaviour!

They laugh, and Miss gives us more jelly beans.
I wonder why kind people always have jelly beans.

CHANGE OF ADDRESS

It's Friday night.
I've survived a second week at school.
I go to feed Tracker
for the last time
at The North Star pub.

In the morning,
I'll collect my not-so-little brown dog,
say goodbye to the past,
and take him with us to
14, Woodcutter's Road.

DARKNESS CLOSES IN

14, WOODCUTTER'S ROAD

We moved in today,
feel at home right away,
at 14, Woodcutter's Road.

The grass is quite long
but there's nothing else wrong,
at 14, Woodcutter's Road.

It's quite a big place,
we've got so much space,
at 14, Woodcutter's Road.

We sit having tea,
Mum, Beth and me,
at 14, Woodcutter's Road.

A new chapter begins
and we all sit and grin,
at 14, Woodcutter's Road.

And Tracker is here
with all of his gear,
at 14, Woodcutter's Road.

CALLING FOR PRECIOUS

It's Monday morning.
I call for Precious, so we can walk together
to Spencer's Wood Academy.

It's easier to walk through the gates
with a friend,
a friend called Precious
who's a bit like
a friend called Roxy.

We always take the long route
to our classroom, so we don't have to go past
T1
K1
W1
You know why.

We put stuff we don't need in lockers, outside M1,
take the long route to the library, so we don't go past
W1
K1
T1
You know why.

It's easier to come to school, be at school,
with a friend,
a friend called Precious
who's a bit like
a friend called Roxy.

AN IMPORTANT JOB

Mrs Reynolds says,
I have an important job for you today!
I can feel myself grow taller.
I want to have a book sale at lunchtimes, she explains,
some of our old books have been replaced
by new editions, so we'll sell the old copies.
Precious, can you keep the display tidy?
Ava, can you take the money? Here's the float.

Yes, Miss! we chorus together,
almost standing to attention,
as if we're in Mrs Reynolds' army,
as if we're wearing crisp uniforms
only worn by the chosen few.

And I think I can hear a million hands clapping
inside the books, that stand to attention on the shelves.
I can hear a million feet marching with me,
as I stride in step to a new story,
with a plot of my choosing.

GRENADES

We've run the sale all week,
most books have been sold,
and now that it's Friday,
we count up the money,
feel proud of our hard work.

The library is full at lunchtime.
Precious tidies some shelves,
I'm at the counter, guarding the float,
when the door swings open wide and
Shafiq and Theo strut through.

Mrs Reynolds is at the other end, so
Precious joins me behind the counter.
Theo knocks the display, books tumble.
This place is a mess! he sniggers.
Got any books about homeless people?

I can't march on with my head held high.
Grenades of malice are being thrown,
and my ears ring with exploding words.
So this is why you're never outside –
we really miss you! gibes Shafiq.

Theo pretends to read a book,
Shafiq barges past Precious and me
to sit behind the counter, smirking.
My mouth is dry, my stomach churning.
This is the wrong story, the wrong plot.

You're not allowed behind here! I snap,
as Shafiq jangles the float tin in the air.
Who says so, Booking.com, who says so?
I SAY SO! shouts Mrs Reynolds. *I SAY SO!*
Taking the enemy completely by surprise.

i WANTED TO SAY . . .

When Dad shouted at Mum,
I wanted to say, *Leave her alone!*
But I didn't.

When others hogged the hotel kitchen,
I wanted to say, *It's for us, too!*
But I didn't.

When Theo called me Booking.com,
I wanted to say, *I've moved!*
But I didn't.

I've noticed that days are often
made up of things I didn't say,
but wanted to.

W1 AND M1 HAVE GAMES

W1 and M1 have Games last two lessons on Friday.
It's a horrible end to the week, I hate every minute,
because Grace and Lucy are in W1, so I have to
watch my back, look out for any unexpected, covert
attacks.

They often play games with me in the changing room,
even before we go out to the field – and I always lose.
Today they've taken my school bag. They empty it
onto the floor, read Mr Amir's poem, laugh. Lucy
pockets it.

They start to throw my spare locker key to each
other, until Miss Jones rushes over, tells them to
repack my bag,
tells them to say sorry, that she will tell Mr Wilson.
There's no place for bullying at Spencer's Wood! she
says.

And all I can see is darkness, as I slowly plod back
to M1.
But when I reach the classroom door, Lucy and
Grace are already waiting.

They say sorry, give me my spare locker key.
You left this in the changing rooms, says Lucy, grinning.

Painting My Room

It's a dull and drizzly Saturday, but
we're painting my room sky-blue
and Nana has come to help us.

It's hard to see in some corners,
so Mum gets a desk lamp
and shines it like a spotlight.

After we've had a tea break
Nana says, *Can I have the lamp,*
I've just painted the carpet!

I move the lamp, it lights her face,
and for a moment we just stare
and then we giggle into song –

This little light of mine
I'm gonna let it shine
Oh, this little light of mine
I'm gonna let it shine
This little light of mine
I'm gonna let it shine

Let it shine
Let it shine
Let it shine.

Mum joins in on the second time.

We have fish and chips for tea,
and when Nana has to go
she hugs the breath out of me!

TRACKER'S PAINT BRUSH

After Nana has gone, we find

brush strokes
of
paint
on
the
stairs
on
the
TV
on
the
bedroom
doors,

then we find Tracker in the garden,
painting the plants with his sky-blue tail.

SUNDAY NIGHT

My room is looking great,
but there's no time to wait
for the smell of drying paint to disappear.

So I'm sharing Mum's big bed,
laying down my weary head,
and trying to calm down my Monday fears.

Yet with every tick and tock
I hear from the bedroom clock,
I feel Monday morning getting very near.

But Precious will be there,
and fear is halved when shared,
like problems, when you need your head to clear.

So I turn and snuggle down,
think of how her giggles sound
when they tickle and rebound inside my ears!

DISCOVERING THE ENEMY CAMP

Precious' giggles are tickling and rebounding in my ears.
I called for her at 8.30, so we don't have to rush to school.

As we round the corner of Woodcutter's Road, I freeze and
step back – the ice of fear numbs my brain, pauses breath.

What's wrong? asks Precious, urgently. *Shh!* I whisper, as I lock onto her eyes. *It's THEM,* I say, in hushed tones.

Precious looks around the corner, sees Aleesha, Grace, Lucy,
sitting on a low wall outside a house in Wood Hill Road.

I push my body into movement, look around the corner again.
The girls are laughing and shrieking, wanting to be heard.

The front door of the house opens, and Shafiq strides out.
The front door of the next house opens, Theo emerges.

We've discovered the enemy camp, almost stumbled into it.
I can see their houses and mine from the same street corner!

Don't panic, encourages Precious, *we'll go past the shops,*
it's only a couple of minutes longer to walk to school.

Soon we're near the school gates, only a few steps to go,
when a jeering voice calls, *Hey, Booking.com, slow down!*

The five of them race towards us, like cold, sleek missiles
locked onto a target, on a mission of terror and destruction.

I need to put a shield up, stop their sneering spite in its track.
I need to defend myself, to stand firm with my head held high.

You can't call me that, I say, with a sneer of my own, *I've moved from the hotel. I live in a house . . . with a garden!*

They stand without an answer, until Aleesha asks where.
She won't tell us, claims Shafiq, *but we'll find out.*

WE NEED TO HAVE A TALK

Girls, I'm glad you're here,
we need to have a talk,
says Mrs Reynolds, firmly.
Did you lock the float tin
in the office on Friday?
It's completely disappeared!

I feel my cheeks heating up,
a blush creeps over my face.
Ava always remembers to,
replies Precious, watching me
struggle, as I trawl my memory –
fishing for an answer.

I can't remember, I confess,
uncomfortable with my reply.
I think I did, but it was busy
and those boys caused trouble
and we had to tidy up the
books they'd knocked to the floor!

We'll talk about it again at Break,
says Mrs Reynolds, *we'll do a search.*
But, in her voice, I hear suspicion,
like when Dad used to question me,
when I knew I was innocent, but
he made me feel guilty.

ONLY ME

We go to the library at Morning Break.
Mrs Reynolds sends me to Mr Daniels –
only me.

I stand outside the door, look at the sign
HEAD TEACHER. No one else is here,
only me.

Ten minutes later, after I've been stared at
by teachers and pupils, the door opens, I go in,
only me.

He asks me how I'm settling in, am I happy.
Says he likes to ask how all his pupils are, not
only me.

I hear the library float tin has disappeared.
Do you know where it might be? he asks
only me.

Is money tight at home, Ava? he enquires.
You can talk to me about problems, he suggests to
only me.

And I look at my knees and try not to cry, knowing the search for the thief has been narrowed down to only me.

WITNESS FOR THE PROSECUTION

Mum arrives, with Noah and Max
balanced on her slim hips.
Mr Thomas enters the courtroom, too,
looking sombre.

Questioning begins, is efficient,
so Mum holds my hand, strokes my arm,
signals solidarity, yet fidgets in her chair
because she remembers well,
my regular cake-stealing phase.

Shafiq enters, standing tall,
eyes as wide as a Disney character's peepers.
Mr Thomas asks,
Shafiq, is this the girl you told me you saw
with the float tin?
Shafiq nods, looks serious.
I begin to ask myself if I did take it,
doubting my own sanity.

Any evidence? asks Mum, as she grips
my hand tighter. Mr Daniels looks at her.
Can we open Ava's locker?
Is that okay?

THE ESCORT

I march
behind
adults,
arms
swaying
in time,
until we
reach the
lockers.

I know
they won't
find the
float tin
because
I didn't
take it.
We stop
marching,

now we spread out in a semi-circle
around my
metal locker.

Mrs Murphy,
my form teacher,
joins us for the spectacle.
I feel euphoric,
because justice will be done,
Mum will be proud
– light will shine in the darkness.

DARKNESS CLOSES IN

Inside my locker,
they find an empty float tin.
Darkness closes in.

My eyes lose focus,
the world comes to a standstill.
Darkness closes in.

My mind spins round fast
like dust in a tornado.
Darkness closes in.

And Mum is crying,
her disappointment showing.
Darkness closes in.

I have no defence
in the face of evidence.
Darkness closes in.

Suspended, they say,
then a meeting on Monday.
Darkness closes in.

i KNOW SHE KNOWS

On Tuesday, Beth calls at 14, Woodcutter's Road.
She asks me how I'm settling in at my new school,
but she really wants to ask me about the float tin.
I know she knows.

She makes a fuss of Tracker, tickles his soft tummy.
*He's getting **so** big!* she says. *He's one **big** brown dog!*
We talk about the house, not about the float tin, but
I know she knows.

After a while, she asks about the float tin, it's a relief.
I tell her I didn't take it, didn't put it in my locker.
I tell her I wouldn't do that to Mrs Reynolds, and
I know she knows.

She asks me to tell her everything that happened.
I tell her about the sale, the bullies, Games, the
shock. I tell her I don't know what to do.
She smiles, and
I know she knows.

WITNESSES FOR THE DEFENCE

The meeting at school has been moved to today, Friday. Beth has been chatting to some of my teachers, 'unofficially'.

She tells me Miss Jones doesn't think
I would steal a float tin, and

Mrs Reynolds says it'd be completely
out of character and that
I went to Games from the library.

Mrs Murphy saw me outside M1
straight after Games,
says I definitely didn't open my locker.

Miss Jones says Lucy and Grace
were throwing my locker key to each other.

Mrs Murphy says they're friends with Shafiq.

THE PLOT HAS **THICKENED**.

When we get to school,
Mr Daniels welcomes us at the door –
asks Mum if she'd like a coffee,
offers me squash and biscuits.

He has spoken to Lucy, Grace and Shafiq.
The girls blame Shafiq,
he blames the girls.
Theo and Aleesha keep out of it, hide.

The case for the prosecution falls apart,
my accusers apologise.

I'm invited to stay at school,
but I prefer to go home today.
The sunlight is gentle on our backs,
the twins sleep in the buggy.
Mum says, *I'm so sorry.*
We think our own thoughts all the way home.

BRIGHT FLARES OF HOPE

IGNORED AND ADORED

I spend the next few weeks being ignored
by Shafiq, Theo, Aleesha, Grace and Lucy.

I spend the next few weeks being adored
by the teaching staff at Spencer's Wood.

Not sure which is the weirdest experience!

THEOPHILOUS

The day before half-term,
there's a chant in the playground,
but it isn't, *Booking.com, Booking.com*.

Theophilus, Theophilus
A name that is preposterous!
Theophilus, Theophilus
A name that is preposterous!

Theo has made a mistake.
He has explained his full name is
Theophilus.

It sounds like a name you'd give a monster!
shrieks Aleesha, and they all laugh.

Theophilus, Theophilus,
a name that is so monster-ous!
Theophilus, Theophilus,
a name that is so monster-ous!

He has provided his friends
with a new thing to mock,
and it's very hard for him
not to feel mocked himself.

Everyone starts to crowd around,
watching the four of them turning
on one of their own, on their friend.

Why did your parents give you
such a weird name? asks Shafiq.

It's not weird in Greece! Theo shouts,
brushing away a tear with the back of his hand.

Actually, Theophilus means 'divine gift',
I say, determined not to hide,
so that makes it a brilliant name.

Everyone freezes. It's as if the whistle has gone!
And then it does.

WALKING HOME

We see Theo
in front of us
walking home
alone.
We catch up
with him.
Precious asks,
Where are the
others,
your friends?
Don't know,
don't care!
spits Theo,
angrily.

We let him
walk ahead,
slowing
our pace
to the lilt
of this bright
October
afternoon.

Suddenly,
Theo turns,
stares at me.
Thank you,
he says,
softly.

OCTOBER MORNING

Tracker snuggles next to me in bed,
his legs stick up, defying gravity.
I rest my face against his soft brown head.

And even when my days are tinged with dread,
on mornings when I'd really like to flee,
Tracker snuggles next to me in bed.

I sigh and smile cos half-term is ahead,
I stroke his ears and whisper, *I am free*.
I rest my face against his soft brown head.

He's loyal like the dogs in books I've read,
whenever I feel down – a nobody –
Tracker snuggles next to me in bed.

His body is as long as mine, when spread,
his coat is wild and choppy, like the sea.
I rest my face against his soft brown head.

And this October morning, brown and red,
seems reflected in the colours next to me.
Tracker snuggles next to me in bed,
I rest my face against his soft brown head.

THE LIE OF SAFETY IN NUMBERS

At the end of a warm but windy Tuesday,
we're having a sleepover – Precious and me.
We share deep secrets,
thoughts that have to be handled with care,
thoughts that would be dangerous
if they fell into the wrong hands,
fell into the wrong minds.

Tracker listens in. I think our secrets are safe.

After a settled silence, I ask a question.

Do you think they've made friends again, the 5 of them?

Precious thinks for a while.

Probably. They think there's safety in numbers, she replies.

Silence.

A few minutes later, I turn over, curl up ready to sleep.

I like the number 2, I yawn.

Feels safe to me, sighs Precious.

Silence.

Sleep.

JUST A BOY IN THE PARK

I need my coat on Friday.
Despite the threat from rainclouds,
Tracker needs a walk, and so do I.

With Precious away, visiting her aunty,
it's just the two of us,
me with my thoughts,
Tracker with dog thoughts.

As we go through the park gate,
I see a boy,
pushing backwards and forwards
on one of the swings,
his feet never leaving the ground.

His collar is up, his hat pulled down low.
He stares at the leaves pooling around his feet,
watches them fly away with a gust of wind.

Tracker growls.

Don't be unfriendly, Tracker, that's not like you!

I pull on Tracker's lead – he won't move.

I stare back at the boy, notice loose, black curls
bubbling out from his hat, around his neck.

Shafiq.

Today, Shafiq doesn't look safe.
He's a 1 not a 5. He's just Shafiq,
just a boy in the park.

Tracker is pulling away, but I stroke him, tell him to come,

drag

him

behind

me.

Salty white lines from cried tears stain Shafiq's face.

He's not aware of our approach.

We stop a few metres away from him.

Tracker growls again.
Shafiq looks up.

I don't know what to expect next.

Shafiq just droops his head again.

My heart beats faster.

He looks small, defeated, abandoned.

He looks like darkness is closing in on him.

You okay, Shafiq?

Words explode from his lips. *What do you care!*
Tracker cowers.

I walk slowly towards him, stroking Tracker in case he growls again.
I sit on the swing next to him, and Tracker sits at my feet
with his head on my lap.

Silence.

Is that your dog now, he asks after a while, *not just your 'friend'?*

I'm allowed one now we live in a house, now we've moved to Spencer's Estate.

Shafiq looks startled.

You live on my estate?

Yeah, just around the corner from you. Can't believe you didn't know!

There's a lot of things I don't know, he sighs.

I sit with him until the wind gets spiteful, throws dust in our faces.

I'm going home before it rains. You should, too, I suggest, *you'll get drenched.*

Who would care? he mumbles into his chest.

I would, I say.

UNEXPECTED VISITOR

I'm sitting at the lounge table,
trying to get the homework done
we've been given for half-term.

I did tell you not to leave it,
grumbles Mum, sighing hard,
you've only got today and Sunday!

She busies herself in the kitchen,
only stops to open the door
when it's knocked hesitantly.

I hear Shafiq's voice, see his face
poke around the lounge door.
He asks, *You done the maths set?*

We talk about the questions
we've both not answered.
It's not what he wants to talk about.

After half an hour of talking about
things he doesn't want to talk about,
Shafiq asks, *Is it hard without your dad?*

Tears slowly slip down his cheeks.
Dad has left my mum, left us. He sobs,
talks and talks, hardly taking a breath.

I make room for his tears to fall,
leave the gaps empty, vacant,
just let him do some quiet sitting.

Then, I tell him about my dad leaving –
about the problems and the hurting.
Tell him that things get better.

THE PROBLEM WITH MATHS

I finish my maths,
late Saturday night.

The problem with maths is
there are too many problems to solve.

A bit like life,
only with numbers.

SHAFIQ COMES FOR A WALK

Tracker's paws trot through the autumn leaves,
the lightness of his touch creates a dance.
My boots tread heavily the path he's stepped,
this Sunday afternoon around the park.
Ava! rings a voice from the park gate,
I turn, and Shafiq races down the path.
We walk and talk until the words run out,
then return to the estate where we both live.
I know he'll find it hard when school begins,
when people ask him why his dad has gone.
I know he'll find it hard on Father's Day,
if he doesn't get a visit from his dad.

He says that, though his dad's not coming back,
the darkness in his head is not so black.

THE SECOND NOTE

On Sunday night, we hear the letterbox snap
its vicious jaws. The postman keeps his fingers.

I go to pick up the random junk that will have fallen,
but only one envelope looks up at me, with my name
on it.

I sit on the stairs,
unstick the flap,
prise it open.

I pull out
a sheet
of A4 lined paper and read –

Hi Ava,

We thought you'd like to have this back.

Sorry,

Shafiq, Theo, Aleesha, Grace and Lucy X

I feel something else
in the envelope,
an older piece of paper,
a bit tattered and torn.
I know this piece of paper.
I unfold it, gently, lovingly,

There was a young lady called Ava,
Who loved every jelly bean flavour.
She took some to school,
Made the other kids drool –
What terribly shocking behaviour!

I don't know whether to laugh or cry.

GLIMMERS

Even in darkness,
Sunday night is full of light.
Glimmers of hope shine.

THE DIFFERENCE IN SMILES

The next half-term
quickly leads us
towards Christmas.

It's an uneventful
time – ordinary,
and I'm grateful.

When Shafiq sees me
he smiles widely, talks,
sometimes for ages.

When Theo, Aleesha,
Grace and Lucy see me
they flash narrow smiles.

When teachers see me,
they nod approval,
still smile apologies.

None of the smiles
can match Nana's
warm, glowing beam.

THE INVITATION

On the last day of term
we break up at lunchtime.
Precious is clearing out her locker,
so I stand with her.
I don't really use mine now.

I see the big 5 strutting up
the corridor towards us.
Lucy speaks for them all.
Next term, we'd like you 2
to hang out with us more.

THE REFUSAL

Thanks for the invitation,
I reply, genuinely touched,
but we work best as a 2,
the rules are more simple.
Can we just be friends?

They all nod in unison
slip past us, awkwardly.
Theo, the girls, still smile narrow smiles.
Shafiq lags behind, turns,
See you later? he asks.

CHRISTMAS CARDS

At home, I read the Christmas cards given to me at school.
16! That's more than I got at Beavers Brook Primary, last year!

I arrange them around the walls of my bedroom, count them again,
just in case I've counted some twice, then lie on my bed.

Of course, a very large brown dog is lying next to me.
I glance from one card to the next, naming my friends –

Adam Mustafa Precious Mia Nathan Lily

Stacey Uzma

Emily Milo

Milly Jasper Jack Keeley Brandon Armed

The big 5 don't send Christmas cards, either on religious grounds
or just because they can't cross the boundaries they've set in stone.

I gave a card to Shafiq at school. He put it in his pocket, quickly,
promptly extinguished his wide smile – but he knew I'd seen it.

VISITING MR AMIR

Nana is staying with us this Christmas.
She cooked dinner on Christmas Day –
it was delicious – apart from the sprouts.

Today, the one after Boxing Day, without
a name or a purpose, we're catching the
number 38 bus, so we can visit Mr Amir.

Mum will stay at home with Noah and Max,
Tracker will come with us to enjoy the smells
of memory, to mark familiar spots of belonging.

Mr Amir doesn't know that we're coming.
He leaps off his stool, races round the counter,
picks me up and twirls me round, dizzily happy.

Ava, I've missed you! What brings you here?
He shakes Nana's right hand with both of his,
then ruffles Tracker's coat, enthusiastically.

Come and have a cup of tea, he insists,
I'll close the shop for lunch, business is slow.
And he's right, it's like a ghost town, deserted.

I tell him about the new house, the new school,
and my new friends. Nana interrupts, sometimes,
to tell him how brave I've been, how proud she is.

When we leave, he gives Tracker a dog treat and
parcels up some carrots, broccoli and apples for Nana.
He gives me enough jelly beans to fill a sports stadium!

Make sure you come to see me again, he orders,
as he opens up the old shop door to let us out.
And I know that we will – some things never change.

DISTANT FIREWORKS

WHOOSH!

BANG!

GLITTER

December explodes into January.
Nana will go home in the morning.
Four days later, a new term starts
at Spencer's Wood Academy.

I'm looking forward to seeing
my friends, to walking with
Precious. Looking forward to
being a helpful library nerd.

WHOOSH!

BANG!

GLITTER

Look out the window, Nana! I exclaim,
The sky is full of light, it's beautiful!
Mum sits huddled with Noah and Max
and Tracker, stroking them in turn.

That's what you call a show, Ava,
some money has gone into that!
But remember, smiles Nana,
a bright light can grow from a small match.

ABOUT THE AUTHOR

Coral Rumble is a popular, award-winning poet; in 2018 she won the Caterpillar Poetry Prize. She has worked as a poet and performer for many years, and now specialises in writing and performing for children. Coral has had four collections published; her most recent collection *Riding a Lion* was published by Troika in 2020. She has also contributed to around 150 anthologies for children. Coral performs and gives workshops at art centres, museums, bookshops, libraries, theatres and festivals, as well as in schools. Michael Rosen has commented, 'Rumble has a dash and delight about her work'.

You can visit her website www.coralrumble.co.uk

ABOUT THE ILLUSTRATOR

Shih-Yu Lin studied illustration at Cambridge School of Art. Originally from Taiwan he now lives in Manchester. He has illustrated many children's titles published in both Taiwan and China. His first picture book, *An Ordinary Story*, is published by Troika.